Jim Henson's
Muppet Babies
I Can Help!

by Bonnie Worth   illustrated by Tom Cooke

GROLIER

What a day this has been—
running here, running there.

There are blocks scattered everywhere
and toys all over the sofa!
Who will help clean up?

"I can help!" says Kermit.
"I was playing with those things.
I'll stack the blocks.
I'll put away the toys, too."

Just look at all this laundry.
So many clothes to wash!
Who will help sort it
into two piles—
one for light clothes,
one for dark?

"I can help!" says Fozzie.
"Sorting is fun. Light stuff here.
Dark stuff there."

Snack time is over.
And, my, was it yummy!
But what is this?
There are crumbs on the floor
underneath this chair.
Who will help clean them up?

"I can help!" says Piggy.
"I'll sweep up the crumbs
with my little broom and dustpan."

There's a fire truck on the stairs.
There's a bicycle blocking the hallway.
There's trash that needs sorting.
There's a tired Nanny who needs
to take a little rest.
Who will help?

"I can help!" says Rowlf.
"I'll put the fire truck away in the toy box."

"I'll park my bike in the corner,"
says Skeeter.

"I'll sort the trash," says Scooter.
"Plastic here. Newspapers there."

"And we'll all play quietly by ourselves
so Nanny can get some rest," says Kermit.

The sun has set.
The day is almost over.
There are some tired little ones
who need to get ready for bed
without making a big fuss.

"We can help!"
say the Babies.
"We'll put on our pajamas
and brush our teeth
and wash our faces
and get into bed
and wait for our kisses.
We're very tired,
because we've had a
busy day being *good helpers.*"